The
GARDEN
and the
GLEN

LENOX STREET
PRESS

Lenox Street Press LLC
gardenandglen.com

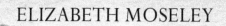

ELIZABETH MOSELEY

The
GARDEN
and the
GLEN

*A Fable about Character
and the Courage to Be Different*

LENOX STREET PRESS

Illustrations by Maggie Green

The GARDEN and the GLEN: A Fable about Character and the Courage to Be Different

Copyright © 2020 by Lenox Street Press LLC.

For information about this title contact the publisher:

Lenox Street Press LLC
P.O. Box 189
Eldred, New York 12732
gardenandglen.com

Library of Congress Control Number: 2019907750

ISBNs
Print: 978-1-7328443-0-8
eBook: 978-1-7328443-1-5

Printed in the United States of America

Cover and Interior design: 1106 Design
Edited by Author Connections, LLC

For Grace, Kathleen, and Caroline,
my inspiration.

For Frank,
my happy ending.

E.M.

CONTENTS

I.

THE GARDEN

IT WAS AN EARLY DAY in summer when everything usual became unusual. The morning was clear and blue. The sky looked like a great, domed ceiling, freshly painted and extending from the mountains to the forest. An old house sat on a hill, above a wide lake surrounded by tall, leafy trees. You could see the house from a mile away in winter, spring, summer, and fall because of its butter-yellow color. There was a vegetable patch next to the house, some apple trees, and a large garden thick with yellow flowers—square beds of sunflowers, snapdragons, buttercups, daisies, and more, spilling over each other and over the yellow fences.

A buckeye tree grew close to the house, unique because of its long, large, pointed yellow flowers that bloomed in spring. On this particular day, the tree was covered in yellow, which was odd to see in the summer season.

A blue butterfly fluttered around the tree. She was beautiful and easy to spot, like a berry in butter.

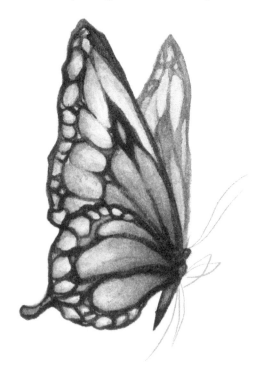

Suddenly, the buckeye started bending from one side to the other and a low, tapping rhythm, like a softly beating drum, came from the tree. Then the crown of the buckeye floated up like a giant yellow cloud. When the bright, noisy cloud rose and moved away, the tree was left quiet with green leaves on dark branches.

The yellow cloud raced around the garden. Up. Down. Left. Right. The blue butterfly appeared slightly ahead of it, and as the drumming grew louder, it revealed a chant, "Be gone. Be gone. You don't belong!" Then the cloud broke into a thousand tiny pieces—yellow butterflies—all chasing the blue one just beyond their reach.

The blue butterfly darted and dashed while the yellow ones zigged and zagged behind her. She slipped between flower petals and leaves while her chasers swarmed in circles. The drumming of their beating wings became louder and a chant became clearer. "She does not belong. It's wrong. It's wrong!"

After a while, her little wings tired and the blue butterfly lost her lead. The yellow butterflies surrounded her, pushing and pulling her up and down. They whirled around her and sent the blue butterfly spinning, twisting and turning out of control and out of the garden.

Once the blue stranger was gone, the yellow butterflies hovered together briefly and then scattered, landing in the garden, where it was impossible to tell the flowers from the butterflies. Then the garden became still, as if nothing had happened.

The Garden

II.

THE GLEN

THE BLUE BUTTERFLY FLEW AWAY as fast as she could. She didn't know if the yellow butterflies were still chasing her, but she flew as if they were. She was afraid to stop. Why did they drive her away? What had she done?

The blue butterfly headed toward the forest to find a safe place to rest. After passing many tall trees, she spotted a clearing with orange daylilies growing around a stream. A small waterfall tumbled over dark rocks, and the blue butterfly saw fish swimming in the stream. She slowed her pace and floated down to hover over the patch of daylilies. The blue butterfly loved their bright color. She was drawn to one in particular, an especially fragrant bloom, and dropped slowly into its soft petals. She drank its sweet nectar and stretched out her six legs.

While perched on the flower, the blue butterfly watched a hummingbird tip his black bill into one of the lilies. His green body and pink throat shimmered in the sunshine. Even with his bright colors, the bird was a silver flash in constant motion.

The hummingbird sensed eyes upon him. The blue butterfly ducked behind the daylily, but too late! The hummingbird darted over to her. "Let me guess. The yellow butterflies don't like you." The blue butterfly was surprised that the bird understood her difficulty.

"How did you know?" she asked.

The hummingbird leaned in and replied, "I know because they did the same to me. I liked to hum around the yellow garden without a care, until one day the garden would only welcome yellow creatures. My pink throat and sparkly green feathers did not blend in, and those yellow butterflies drummed me out of there!" He cocked his head and folded his wings on his back.

While listening to the hummingbird, the blue butterfly noticed a brown squirrel had hopped up on a nearby tree stump. His cheeks were bulging with acorns, but the brown squirrel was determined to tell his story. "Da wewow wutterwies did da wame du we," he said. He stopped to move the nuts to one side of his mouth. "That's better." The brown squirrel began again.

"The yellow butterflies did the same to me. It was in the fall, when I was gathering acorns in the garden. I scooted by what I thought was a large clump of yellow mums, but the flower tops popped off and attacked me!" The brown squirrel took a breath and moved the nuts once again to the other side of his mouth. "It was the yellow butterflies. I dropped a day's worth of acorns and ran. I still shake a little when I think about it."

Two large green frogs overheard the conversation. They hopped away from the stream and squatted near the orange lilies.

"They did it to us, too," croaked the frogs. "We lived on the lake by the yellow house. The lily pads were our home. This spring, the yellow butterflies came day after day and swooped down on us like winged torpedoes! We couldn't take it! We gave up our home and came over here with our young ones." The bigger frog gestured to four little frogs who hopped out of the stream and onto the low rocks by the waterfall.

A school of rainbow trout poked their heads out of the stream. One by one, they jumped and flashed their sparkling colors. The biggest trout swam over to the blue butterfly.

"We also had a good life in that lake. The flies were plentiful and we ate well. One day, the yellow butterflies circled over the lake, made lots of noise, and scared the flies away. They did it over and over until the flies stopped coming. I brought my family here so we wouldn't go hungry." The colorful fish puckered his lips, turned, and swam away.

"Don't forget me!" A cardinal sailed down and hopped nervously about the forest floor. When they saw him, the other creatures encouraged the red bird to tell the blue butterfly about his experience. The cardinal flew to a low pine branch and bounced around until he found a comfortable spot.

"Clearly, I did not blend in!" he chirped with a hint of sadness. "I helped my mate build a nest behind the yellow house. It's a lot of work to build a nest—constant back and forth for little twigs and fluff." The cardinal took a deep breath. "We had three eggs about to hatch. I was gathering some dry moss when I heard the sound of wings tapping. The yellow butterflies flew into the nest and used their wings to bump and push our eggs! My mate and I fought them off until our little ones hatched and were ready to fly." The cardinal looked up and smiled at his young family perched in the tree.

The blue butterfly studied her new neighbors. Their shapes and colors were all different. They didn't look or talk like she did. "I'm so small in comparison," the blue butterfly thought, "yet they included me. They certainly didn't chase me away!"

Together, they watched the sky turn from bright day to evening shade with streaks of pink and gold. Before long, the colors grayed into darkness. The glow of the silver moon cast a cool light, and a cluster of stars twinkled above them.

The blue butterfly felt safe with her new friends. "Thank you for turning this into a good day," she said, "and a good night."

The hummingbird hummed, "Goodnight," and flew over near the waterfall.

The brown squirrel squeaked, "Goodnight," and scurried up the nearby oak tree.

The frogs croaked, "Goodnight," and hopped over the rocks into the stream. Four little splashes followed close behind.

The trout bobbing in the current gurgled, "Goodnight," before darting down into the dark water.

The cardinal sang, "Goodnight," and snuggled into his nest.

The blue butterfly drew another long sip from the daylily and sank comfortably into the flower's welcoming petals. She folded her wings and let out a slow, sad sigh. "Goodnight and thank you for the food and place to rest. I'll miss you."

"Where am I going?" asked the daylily, with a smile.

"The flower of a daylily lasts only for one day," replied the blue butterfly.

The lily bent her flowered head, curled her soft petals around her new friend, and yawned, "Goodnight. Let's see what tomorrow brings."

III.

THE QUEEN

THE DAY WAS NOT YET DONE for the yellow butterflies. They returned to the buckeye tree and stacked on top of each other, covering the trunk and branches. Moonlight washed over the tree, and the buckeye looked like it was wearing a thick, yellow coat. Thousands of wings were open wide. There was no flying, swarming, tapping, or chanting. There was no drumming. It was quiet on the tree. The butterflies were awaiting word of their Queen.

The Butterfly Queen was known far and wide as a sensible, smart, and caring leader. She was the reason

the blue butterfly had come to the garden in the first place. Butterflies of every color, size, and shape were welcome to flutter and feed from the variety of plants and flowers in her queendom. The blue butterfly wanted to live in such a place, but before she arrived, the Queen had become sick. That's when everything changed.

The Queen rarely left her throne room. She was too weak to pay attention to her queendom. In her absence, a newcomer to the garden had taken control. He was yellow in color and larger than the others. He was also very bossy.

The bossy butterfly frightened the members of the garden community and threatened them if they didn't do what he wanted. He wanted the queendom—with its diverse wildlife and colorful plants and flowers—to be one color. He wanted everything everywhere to be like him. He ruled that only yellow flowers and plants could grow in the garden, and all the butterflies and creatures that were not yellow had to be chased away. The bossy butterfly had plans to turn the queendom into his yellow kingdom, but first he needed the Queen out of the way.

Through it all, a wise butterfly—the Queen's physician and advisor—remained loyal. He didn't trust the new leader. He wanted the Queen well and in charge again. He had tried numerous remedies, but nothing worked. The wise butterfly was baffled and anxious as the Queen grew weaker.

The wise butterfly came from a long line of healers tasked with the protection and well-being of the butterfly order. Up until now, his use of mineral waters and herbal remedies had proven effective in curing the ills of his winged patients. The wise butterfly realized the Queen's ailment demanded extraordinary measures. Her condition called for magic.

Later that night, he told the Queen about the legend of the medicine flower.

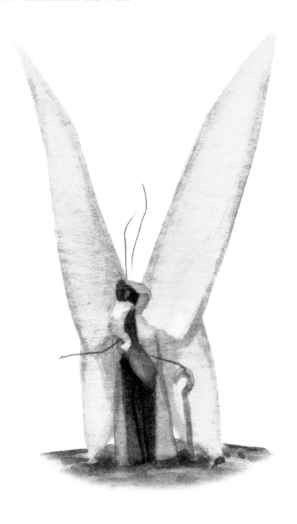

IV.

THE BOSS

THE YELLOW BUTTERFLIES WERE gathered on the buckeye tree. Their pale and feeble Queen appeared and cautiously mounted her throne at the top. She gestured to the wise butterfly, and he came forward. He sipped at the cool night air, stepped into a moonbeam, and addressed the crowd. "My friends, I am convinced we must do more to save our Queen and restore her good health." The wise butterfly looked back at the Queen. She encouraged him with a smile, and he returned to his remarks.

"In every garden there is one medicine flower that contains a fragrant, healing potion. The magical liquid flows up through the stem to the blossom's center. It exists for all the butterflies, who help the flowers grow and multiply. There is a medicine flower in the Queen's garden."

Before he could continue, the bossy butterfly jumped up from a low branch and flew around the buckeye, clapping his wings and clicking his six legs together until all the butterflies were looking at him. Disregarding the Queen and the wise butterfly, he addressed the large assembly:

"Our Queen's health is failing, and I have the solution!" He thought for a few moments, then continued, "If the Queen drinks the potion from the medicine flower, she will be well again!" He tried to sound happy, but it was hard for him. The bossy butterfly was angry. He hadn't planned on a flower that could save the Queen. He needed to make sure that would never happen. The bossy butterfly flew up to the throne.

"At sunrise, I will fly to the garden and locate the magic flower while the Queen's attendants prepare her for the flight. I will perch on the medicine flower with my wings spread wide. The Queen will see me, land on the flower, drink the potion, and her health will be restored immediately." The bossy butterfly smiled. As usual, he was scheming, and he thought himself very clever.

The Queen did not regard the bossy butterfly as clever. She thought he was rude and disrespectful. He had ignored her presence, interrupted her wise counsel, and held court with her subjects. Unfortunately, she couldn't protest. Weak and tired, her noble head hung low under the weight of her gold crown. The royal attendants rushed forward and ushered the Queen back to bed.

The bossy butterfly quickly took the Queen's place on the throne, looking down at thousands of eyes staring up at him. He liked being high on the tree with the moonlight shining on him. He smiled again, knowing his scheme would exhaust the Queen even further and cast doubt on the wise butterfly's foolish legend.

With the Queen soon out of the way, he would be King. Then he would make everything, everywhere exactly the same.

V.

THE BULLY

THE NEXT MORNING, the bossy butter-
fly flew through the garden, pretending to search
for the medicine flower. In a short time, he grew
tired and hungry, and decided he had looked busy
long enough. He landed atop a yellow daisy to rest,
stretched his wings wide, and daydreamed of being
King. Certainly, he would have a bigger crown!

While he imagined his future glory, the Queen
flew overhead. She looked for the bossy butterfly
but could not see him because he and the daisy

were the same color. His wings blended with the flower and completely disappeared.

The Queen passed over several more times without spotting him. She shook her head in disappointment. "The bossy butterfly is a show-off, yet when I need him to show himself the most, he is nowhere to be found!" She circled the garden a final time before flying back to her roost at the top of the tree.

Upon her return, the weary Queen was escorted to her chamber inside the buckeye. The wise butterfly remained outside her throne room and explained the misadventure to the others. "It was a bad plan all along. How could the Queen find the potion flower? One yellow butterfly atop a yellow flower among thousands of yellow flowers is impossible to spot!" The wise butterfly shook his antennae slowly. "We cannot save the Queen if she can't see us." The other butterflies nodded their heads and flapped their wings in agreement.

The bossy butterfly returned to the tree and overheard the complaints. He circled, dipping and darting among the branches. He landed and opened his wings, pushing two yellow butterflies out of the way. Then he addressed the assembly in his loudest and bossiest tone.

"Being all the same is absolutely right! We are fiercer and more frightening united as one!" He waved his wings dramatically. "Look how the yellow garden we've created matches the yellow house. Now, the fences match the garden. Everything matches, everything is the same. That is how it should be!"

The bossy butterfly looked up from his perch in the middle of the tree and saw all eyes were on him. Then he looked down and caught sight of a ladybug crawling on the ground below. Though very small, her bright red shell was sharply visible against the yellow flowers.

The bossy butterfly had a thought and raised his voice again. "Remember that blue butterfly we chased out of the garden?" The antennae of all the butterflies waved up and down. "Together, we were like a giant broom. We swept that blue outsider away. She did not belong!" The bossy butterfly loved the sound of his own voice and the fear it inspired, but this time his loud, angry speech disturbed the Queen. She rose from her bed and leaned against the chamber door to listen.

Mention of the earlier incident gave the wise butterfly an idea. "What if the blue butterfly was atop the medicine flower?" he said out loud. Right away, all eyes turned in his direction. He continued, "Surely the Queen would see the blue butterfly. Her blue wings would stand out against the yellow flowers and guide the Queen to the potion!"

The bossy butterfly stiffened his antennae. His head twitched as he watched the yellow butterflies flapping their wings and nodding.

"The blue butterfly could be the solution to our problem, but we don't know where she is or if she'll help us after the way she's been treated here," the wise butterfly said. He shrugged his wings and shook his head.

VI.

A TRAP

THE BOSSY BUTTERFLY STOPPED twitching. His antennae relaxed. He was thinking, as he often did, about a way to benefit himself without doing any work. Calmly and quietly, he circled the yellow buckeye. He didn't interrupt; he didn't demonstrate his usual lack of self-control. He landed softly at the end of a long branch.

Addressing all the butterflies, he spoke in a superior tone. "You should find the blue butterfly and apologize," he said, tapping his wings together under his chin.

The wise butterfly stared in disbelief. "WE should apologize?" The wise butterfly shook his cane at the bossy butterfly and continued, "The blue butterfly is not here to help us because YOU drove her away. YOU wanted everything to be the same!"

The bossy butterfly's antennae whirled in a circle above his head. Without warning, he charged the wise butterfly and sent him spinning in the air.

The wise butterfly dropped to a lower branch and staggered backwards, looking about for his cane. Unconcerned, the bossy butterfly flew to the top of the tree and announced, "We must unite for our Queen and find the blue butterfly!" The butterflies rose off the tree like a giant yellow kite. The bossy butterfly muttered to himself, "Everything is falling into place. I will soon be King!"

But as the butterflies waited, the bossy butterfly hesitated. There was movement on the ground below. The little ladybug was still working her way across the garden. She moved steadily toward her home in the yellow roses.

Certain all the butterflies were watching, the bossy butterfly swooped down and wildly flapped his wings. The frightened ladybug was tossed in the air and landed upside down on her shiny red polka dot shell. Her legs waved frantically in the sunlight.

The bossy butterfly laughed and then shouted orders. He took the lead and flew toward the forest with the butterflies trailing behind him like long yellow ribbons. He smiled and whispered to himself, "If the blue butterfly's wings can save the Queen, I'll have to get rid of the blue butterfly."

VII.

VISITORS

OVER IN THE GLEN, the blue butterfly warmed herself in the sunshine. The big and little frogs visited with the rainbow trout. The hummingbird hummed from one flower to the next. The cardinal perched on an evergreen branch, cleaning his feathers. The brown squirrel scurried about, collecting nuts by a fallen tree.

A doe and her two fawns jumped—one, two, and three—over the fallen tree. Surprised by their arrival, the brown squirrel dropped all the nuts stuffed in his cheeks. He stamped his feet and brushed his thick, bushy tail back and forth. "Not again!" he said. While he gathered them up, he motioned to the blue butterfly to introduce herself to the visitors.

"No time for introductions!" said a tiny voice coming from the deer trio. A gray bunny with a pink nose was perched between the ears of one of the fawns. "They're coming for you," said the gray bunny to the blue butterfly. "The yellow butterflies are coming." The fawn lowered his head, and the bunny scampered down.

The blue butterfly looked around and saw the brown squirrel tapping his foot. The frogs were shaking their heads while the trout slapped their tails on the water. The hummingbird and cardinal crossed their wings over their chests and pointed their beaks up in the air. The gray bunny was known for "crying wolf," spreading false alarms and scaring the glen community.

The squirrel spoke first. "Are you sure about the butterflies, gray bunny? Remember when you told me the mossy log floating in the stream was an alligator?" There was giggling and gurgling.

The hummingbird hummed back and forth before announcing, "The first day I met gray bunny he was hiding in the ferns. He told me a storm was coming. There was no storm; he was hiding from the sound of the waterfall!"

Then, it was the trout's turn. "I recall gray bunny alerting me to a bear cub crawling along in the shallows at night. The bear turned out to be a beaver, working on his lodge." All the woodland creatures laughed and croaked even louder.

The gray bunny wrinkled his nose and tore at a leaf of wild cabbage. He sat back on his hind legs and addressed the group. "This time it's true! I saw the butterflies and heard them, but they didn't see me. I always try to blend in by staying close to the gray stone wall around the vegetable patch. I worry if the yellow butterflies spot me, they will pick me up and carry me away!"

The largest frog croaked a very loud croak, and the gray bunny snapped his head in the frog's direction. "Yes, yes. Back to the point!" He turned and looked again at the blue butterfly. "The yellow butterflies are looking for you," he said, with a bit of cabbage between his front teeth, "Their Queen is very sick."

Before continuing, the gray bunny's ears stood straight up. The sound of drumming was getting closer. The gray bunny shook uncontrollably and opened his mouth wide. No sound came out, though he formed the words, "*I told you they were coming!*" He hopped into the gray shadow of the fallen log, put his front paws over his head and rolled into a ball, hoping to hide his ears and pink nose.

"The yellow butterflies are coming!" squeaked the brown squirrel, looking for a place to hide. The mother deer leapt toward the forest with her fawns close behind, and all three quickly blended in with the dark trunks of the trees. The cardinal nestled into a patch of bee balm—the wild plants' red color and feathery leaves provided him with the perfect cover. The hummingbird flew between the rocks and waterfall; his shiny feathers looked like part of the fast-moving water. The frogs shrank against some mossy stones, fading into the background. The trout scattered into the watery shadows without a trace.

The brown squirrel hurried toward the blue butterfly and said breathlessly, "You are not blending in. We must blend in!" The blue butterfly fluttered close to the squirrel. She didn't want to hide, but didn't want to endanger the others. What was she to do?

VIII.

HIDING

AT THAT MOMENT, the orange daylily bent her long stem toward the blue butterfly. The blue butterfly was surprised to see the same flower that had fed and sheltered her the night before. The lily opened her petals wide as a dinner plate, then closed them up tight into a bud before they opened again.

The brown squirrel understood. He pushed the blue butterfly toward the flower, urging, "Hurry up! Jump in! No time to waste!" The blue butterfly landed in the open flower and the petals closed around her. The brown squirrel rushed up the large oak, curled his tail, and blended in with the dusky hollow of the tree.

The drumming of the yellow butterflies was soon loud enough to drown out the waterfall. The swarm rushed into the glen looking for the blue butterfly, rolling over every leaf and blade of grass in their search.

They worked most of the day, in spite of the hot sun. The bossy butterfly barked commands while quenching his thirst at the patch of orange daylilies. He landed on the daylily next to the one hiding the blue butterfly and dug his needle-like legs deep into

the flower. After drinking his fill, the bossy butterfly lifted off, carelessly shredding the delicate petals. He shouted more orders, and a long train of yellow wings assembled behind him and took off. In seconds, the sky was clear and the glen was quiet.

Cautiously, the orange daylily opened. As her petals unfurled, the blue butterfly rose up and out of the flower. She looked first for the brown squirrel. He was not visible until he wiggled his tail. He hurried down the oak, zipped across the forest floor, and jumped up on a stump covered with velvety green moss. Next, she saw the pink-and-silvery-green hummingbird whirling away from the waterfall. The red cardinal flew over to an evergreen tree. The frogs jumped off the dark stones and into a pool covered with white lotus flowers.

Hiding

In time, the rest of the forest creatures returned, feeling safe again. The gray bunny hopped away from the log to munch on some violets poking out of the ground. The trout family rose from the bottom of the stream and flashed their rainbow scales in the late afternoon sun. The brown deer and her fawns came out of the woods and stood by some white birch trees.

The blue butterfly studied her friends. Their colors, shapes, and sizes made each of them unique and allowed them to stand out. Their differences made them beautiful. She spread her wings, flew above the clearing and announced, "We belong! We don't have to blend in to belong." The daylily clapped her slender leaves together.

The gray bunny piped up, "What about me? I was right! The yellow butterflies WERE coming!" The forest creatures all agreed. The blue butterfly approached the bunny, who was perched on his back legs. She fluttered slowly and bestowed several butterfly kisses on the bunny's round cheeks.

Late afternoon slipped into evening. The animals and birds nibbled their supper while the fish and frogs

enjoyed a late swim. A chorus of "Goodnight" echoed in the dark glen.

When the blue butterfly approached the patch of daylilies, they were all closed except one. She fluttered above the open flower. The blue butterfly's heart was full. "What a surprise and delight that you were here today, my friend," she said. She landed and tucked her blue wings into the soft petals. Before closing her eyes she whispered, "Goodnight. I am grateful to you." The flower replied, "Goodnight. I am grateful *for* you."

The sky darkened. A full moon rose, waking the stars and sparking a web of light across the sky.

IX.

MISSING

THE NEXT MORNING, the blue butterfly rose early without waking her friends and flew toward the forest entrance. She loved the good Queen and wanted to help, but wasn't sure how to go about it. She headed for the garden, looked back for a doubtful instant, and then kept going.

All the creatures in the glen were up at dawn, finding breakfast around the forest. While chewing on some clover, the gray bunny glanced over at the daylilies. The blue butterfly was not there. He hopped over to the clearing and called out to the deer, "Do you see blue butterfly?" The doe and her fawns stopped grazing. The mother looked up at the leaves and branches. Her fawns poked the grasses and wildflowers. The deer shook their heads.

The gray bunny hopped over to the tall oak and called up to the brown squirrel, dozing in the tree. "Do you see blue butterfly?" The squirrel scampered down the tree and searched around his winter stash, scattering acorns on the forest floor. He looked over at the gray bunny, put his front paws up in the air, and shook his head.

Then, the gray bunny hopped over to the stream. As he leaned over the wet rocks, he slipped and fell into the fast water. The frog family quickly jumped in while the trout circled the bunny. Together, they caught the bunny before he was carried away and pushed him back to the grassy edge. The cold, wet bunny shivered and cried out, "DOES ANYONE SEE BLUE BUTTERFLY?!"

The frogs looked around the banks of the stream as the trout family poked their heads in and out of the water, croaking and gurgling, "She isn't here!"

The gray bunny folded himself into a ball and rocked back and forth in the grass while calling out for the blue butterfly. The cardinal and hummingbird heard his cries and flew above the trees, searching the branches. The blue butterfly wasn't there.

X.

BELONGING

A GENTLE VOICE CALLED, "I can help!" The animals, birds, fish, and frogs looked around. "I'm over here, by the stream. Do you see me?" The group turned their gaze toward the wild daylilies. One of the orange flowers was waving her carrot-colored petals back and forth as she called out, "Over here! I have something to say."

The daylily was quickly surrounded, and she opened her blossom in a big smile. The daylily straightened her main stem and nodded to each member of the small assembly.

"I've lived by the stream a long time, and I've seen changes since blue butterfly arrived." The lily looked up at the two birds perched on the same branch. "When hummingbird came to the glen, he had little interest in cardinal. Now, I watch him pull grasses with his long, pointed beak to feather cardinal's new nest."

The flower used her petal to point at the cardinal and said, "You barely looked at hummingbird when you came here with your chicks. Now, your family sings to him every morning." The two birds moved closer together.

The flower turned toward the mother deer. "At first you passed through the glen with barely a nod. Later,

you made a home here with your fawns. I saw you showing them how to scratch acorns off the ground and roll them over to brown squirrel's winter storage." The deer and her fawns nodded while the flower continued, "Recently, I've noticed brown squirrel jumping on the wild azalea branches and bending them low so your fawns can reach the tasty flowers." The brown squirrel scurried over to the deer trio.

Suddenly, there was loud splashing and croaking. The daylily turned to face the frogs and fish in the stream. "I did not forget you!" She pointed her petal and waved it at the frogs. "When you first arrived in the glen, you gobbled up all the flies in sight. Now, you leave some just above the water for the trout to eat." The frogs snapped their long, sticky tongues and the trout jumped.

The daylily dropped her head to look down at the gray bunny. "It was the fish and frogs that kept you from being carried downstream." The gray bunny nodded and hopped over to the rocks beside the water.

The flower made a curling motion with her leaves, inviting the group to come closer. "You are all different and all perfect, just as you are. Lately, you have become more than that. Now, you reach beyond yourselves, using your differences to help your friends. That is the magic of belonging."

At that point, the gray bunny chimed in, "If blue butterfly is not here with us, she is someplace where she doesn't belong. It isn't easy for her to hide!"

The lily looked down at the bunny and shook her petals. "No, gray bunny. Hiding or trying to blend in is something we do out of fear. Belonging means you don't have to change; you're welcome and accepted as you are. Even if you're by yourself, you're never alone when you belong."

"And"—the daylily turned to each of them as she spoke—"just like all of you help each other, blue butterfly left early this morning for the garden, to try and help the Queen."

The birds cried out, "Oh no!!" The fish jumped and slapped the water. The frogs croaked loudly. The brown squirrel shook his head. The gray bunny covered his ears and hopped in a circle. The deer moved their feet around nervously.

"What's wrong?" asked the lily. "Isn't blue butterfly reaching out, as all of you have done?"

The large trout swam over to the lily. His sleek body sliced through the water. "We helped each other here, in the glen. We're all friends. It's much harder out there."

"That's true," said the lily, "and blue butterfly knows it as well. Though she's the smallest, she is proving that we can be bigger than what scares us."

At that, the animals and birds bent down to talk to the fish and frogs in the stream. There was some humming mixed with croaks and squeaks. After the short huddle, they turned back to the lily. The brown squirrel spoke for all. "We must help our friend."

They all prepared to fly, swim, hop, and leap in the direction of the garden. Just as they were about to leave, the lily held up one petal and said, "Tell blue butterfly I'll be waiting for her."

XI.

LOST AND FOUND

IN ANOTHER PART of the forest, the day started with a scolding. The bossy butterfly was angry at his yellow crew for dozing in the morning sun. They had spent the night in the forest; too tired to fly home to the buckeye after searching all day for the blue butterfly.

The bossy butterfly was disappointed that the small blue intruder continued to outsmart them. He wanted to search the garden, but his troops were worn out, hungry, and slow to respond. The bossy butterfly flew into a rage, poking the butterflies with his pointy legs.

Still, they didn't move. Furious, he took off alone, ordering the yellow butterflies to follow close behind.

The blue butterfly had spent the morning searching for the Queen, then flew toward the lake and looked around the apple orchard. Later in the day, as she passed by a maple tree, she spotted the faint outline of two wings. In a flash, she darted over to find the Queen balanced on a leaf.

"You are unwell, my Queen." The blue butterfly bowed before her. "How can I be of service?"

The Queen took a deep breath and told of the failed attempts to find the medicine flower. She repeated what she'd overheard through her chamber door, confiding to the blue butterfly, "I am running out of time, but your colorful wings can lead me to the remedy in the garden."

The garden looked like many yellow carpets stretched long and wide. No one flower stood out. "It will be dark before long. We'll need daylight for such a huge task," the blue butterfly explained.

It was a short flight to the garden, but the Queen was tired upon landing. The blue butterfly guided her to a safe perch in full view of the blooming plants and set off to find the medicine flower.

XII.

TRUE AND FALSE

THE BOSSY BUTTERFLY FLEW toward the garden. He passed the maple tree, flew over the yellow fence, and spotted the blue butterfly immediately. The bossy butterfly dropped from the sky and shrank into the shadow of a watering can. He watched with delight while the blue butterfly carefully examined the square sections of flowers and plants. "I'll wait for her to locate the medicine flower," he thought, "then I'll take charge!"

While searching, the blue butterfly was drawn to the prize-winning yellow roses. The rose beds were the largest in the garden, and her wings drooped as she surveyed the huge task before her. The bossy butterfly smiled from his hiding place. The blue butterfly was doing all the work.

The flower kingdom watched the blue butterfly as well; they loved the dear Queen and wanted to help. The snapdragons told the daisies, the daisies told the buttercups, and the buttercups told the roses to urge the medicine flower to release her unique fragrance. When she did, the blue butterfly noticed the scent right away. She landed on the medicine rose and was instantly revived. She signaled the Queen by fluttering her blue wings.

Right at that moment, the bossy butterfly crawled out of his dark corner. The sight of the blue wings against the yellow rose put his antennae in a twist! The bossy butterfly flew hard, fast, and straight at the blue butterfly.

XIII.

JUSTICE

THE QUEEN HAD SEEN the blue butterfly's signal. She was gathering her strength to fly when the bossy butterfly streaked past. He didn't notice the Queen, but she saw him set his wings, spin his six legs, and prepare to attack.

The blue butterfly looked over her wing expecting the Queen, but instead she saw three pairs of sharp, spinning legs attached to the charging butterfly. She darted away from the medicine flower, narrowly avoiding impact. The bossy butterfly was not as quick. He crashed into the tall, sturdy rose. His error left him bruised and shaken, but the real damage was to his pride. He pulled himself out of the thorny rosebush.

Once again, the bossy butterfly set the two blue wings in his sights and rushed at top speed. The blue butterfly dipped and turned. The bossy butterfly climbed high and then shot straight down like an arrow. The blue butterfly zigged and zagged until her attacker had to stop and rest.

Draped over a yellow aster, the bossy butterfly mumbled out loud, "I must make sure the Queen never finds the medicine flower. Then I'll have the throne, and soon everything everywhere will be the same!" He prepared to charge again, but just before takeoff, something caught his attention. He thought it was a flower petal floating in the air, but then realized it was the Queen herself!

The bossy butterfly was surprised, but, as always, clever. He waved his ragged wing in the blue butterfly's direction and said, "Dear Queen, I have been so concerned about your health. I was searching for the medicine flower when I came upon this rebel!"

The Queen stared at the bossy butterfly in disbe-lief. "I heard your mumblings. Your only concern is to replace me." She was weak, but her voice was stern. "YOU are the rebel who chased color from my queendom! You bullied my subjects and sent them into hiding. You—BE GONE!" The Queen's word was law. It was useless to protest.

Upon hearing her order, the bossy butterfly began to twitch. He flew up, down, left, right, round and round. He bolted toward the rose bush and bashed the medicine flower repeatedly until most of the petals and leaves were gone. He whirled his legs like an eggbeater, shredding what was left. The rose was so severely damaged, it couldn't create the fragrance or draw the potion up from its core.

The bossy butterfly hovered over the broken stem. His chest heaved and puffed, yet he managed to flash a big smile. The Queen's only hope for recovery was shattered. He would claim the throne for himself. He tapped his wings together under his chin upon hearing a familiar sound—the beating wings of a thousand butterflies rolling across the garden. "My yellow broom is here," he said with a grin.

The throng of yellow butterflies arrived and surrounded the blue butterfly. The drumming grew louder, and she pulled her wings up over her head.

At that moment, the Queen cried out, "STOP! Do not harm her." The yellow butterflies froze in mid-air. Like yellow rain, they dropped from the sky, assembling before the Queen.

The Queen pointed her pale, shaking wing at the bossy butterfly and made her voice as large and loud as she could. "HE is the villain! He took advantage of my illness and schemed to take my throne." The Queen took a deep breath and continued. "The wise butterfly was right. A medicine flower grew here in our garden. Blue butterfly found it and did all she could to help me, but this bossy butterfly

destroyed the medicine flower before I could take the cure."

While the Queen mourned the flower, the bossy butterfly tiptoed backwards out of the rose garden. He was about to lift-off and fly away when the Queen turned to face him. Her voice was barely a whisper, "Be gone. Be gone. You don't belong!"

The yellow butterflies formed a giant yellow broom, just as the bossy butterfly had trained them to do. Batting their wings as fast as they could, the flying broom tumbled and tossed him, brushing the bossy butterfly across the thorny rose beds and out of the garden.

XIV.

COMMUNITY

THE YELLOW BUTTERFLIES THEN turned their attention to the Queen. She stared without expression at the battered medicine flower. The blue butterfly looked toward the forest upon hearing movement and chatter. She turned toward the lake and heard croaking and splashing.

The mother deer leapt out of the dark forest with the brown squirrel on her back. Next came her fawns, one with the gray bunny between his ears. The cardinal and hummingbird were close behind.

The blue butterfly was surprised to see her friends bounding over the stone wall and dashing into the garden. The garden was a fearful place and she admired their daring.

Before she could say anything, the gray bunny hopped down from his perch atop the fawn and announced, "We came to help!" The brown squirrel scurried down from the deer's back while the birds landed on a rose bush.

The blue butterfly turned toward the croaking and splashing. She could see right through the Queen's wings; all of her color was gone and her wings were clear as glass. The Queen was fading away.

The blue butterfly pointed at the broken stem and fallen petals of the yellow rose. "I'm afraid you're too late." She told her friends about the medicine flower and the bossy butterfly. "I don't know what to do. I have failed the Queen." The garden was still.

The brown squirrel broke the silence. "I wish the orange lily was here. She would know what to do." The animals and birds nodded. A loud croaking was heard coming from the lake. The gray bunny turned to the blue butterfly. "I almost forgot. The orange lily said to tell you she is waiting for you by the stream."

The blue butterfly thought for a few moments, then looked up at the sky. The fading sun prompted quick action, and suddenly she knew exactly what to do. She and the Queen took off, calling for the animals, birds, and butterflies to follow close behind.

After flying a short time, the blue butterfly turned to see the Queen losing altitude. She gave a signal and the yellow butterflies surrounded the Queen and buoyed her up. The cardinal and hummingbird flew ahead. The flapping of their wings helped to pull the Queen along.

The glen was soon in sight.

XV.

CELEBRATION

THE BLUE BUTTERFLY PUSHED on toward the large cluster of orange daylilies. Hundreds of them stood at the water's edge, but the blue butterfly knew which one to choose. She darted over to the familiar blossom and stretched across it, just as she'd done on her first day in the glen.

The Queen saw the blue wings amid the large orange patch. Summoning her last bit of strength, she made her way to the lily. The blue butterfly closed her wings, slipped under the Queen, and gently cradled her into the open flower. As the soft petals closed around

the Queen, the blue butterfly joined the gallery of loyal subjects, and a vigil began.

The birds perched on a nearby pine. The animals, fish, and frogs returned quietly. The yellow butterflies landed and silently folded their wings. The blue butterfly flew to a large fern and waited. The glen was silent and cool.

The sun was setting when the daylily finally opened. The blue butterfly and her friends squinted in awe as the radiant Queen emerged. Her broad wings were brilliant gold. Her shiny crown, glistening in the soft light, sat high on her head as she twirled above the clearing, nodding and waving to her cheering subjects below.

The blue butterfly was filled with gratitude. Relief and joy washed over her like sunshine. She smiled, recalling her comment about the flower of a daylily lasting only for one day. "No wonder the lily continued to bloom," she thought. "The orange daylily is a medicine flower! She serves all the butterflies, who help the plants and wildflowers grow. Our humble bloom holds the magic that has saved the Queen."

The Queen flew down and hovered over the daylily. Waving her golden wings, she bestowed butterfly kisses on each petal of the enchanted flower. The lily arched her tall stem and bowed before the Queen. The sounds of jumping, singing, leaping, splashing, and croaking filled the glen.

The Queen floated over to the blue butterfly and landed on a leaf beside her. She spoke in a hushed tone as the blue butterfly bowed her head. The Queen wrapped her wings around her in a long embrace and then flew in a small circle above the blue butterfly. She tightened the circle and released a fine, shimmering mist that showered the blue butterfly in sparkling light.

The yellow butterflies assembled behind the Queen as she bid farewell to her forest friends and flew toward the garden. The queendom would heal with its beloved leader strong again. In time, the Queen would mentor the blue butterfly, her successor to the throne.

Darkness fell at the end of the long summer day. "Goodnight, goodnight," echoed in the forest. The moon was not visible. It was a starless night except for one blue star fluttering over the glen.

EPILOGUE

TODAY, THE GARDEN is teeming with butterflies in every size, shape, and shade. Colorful plants and flowers grow tall with borders of blue forget-me-nots. Orange daylilies line the stone walls around the vegetable patch.

The old yellow house remains, surrounded by trees and hills above the lake where fish and frogs live and play. The fences around the apple orchard have toppled, and the deer feed on the fallen fruit. The trees drop plenty of nuts for the squirrels. Hummingbirds drink from brightly colored blooms while cardinals feast on seeds from the sunflowers. Cabbages grow near the buckeye tree for the bunnies. All are welcome. All belong.

In the evening, the creatures look to the western sky and watch for streaks of gold and pink around the setting sun. The sky turns violet, then gray. The moon rests in the dark blanket of the night. Stars wink to all below.

Somewhere, a blue butterfly whispers, "Goodnight."